Sundance Springs Series

M·A·S·H

written & illustrated by
Mary Ann Jensen

SUMMARY: Goodbye middle school! Hello life! I'm Victoria Hemmingsbird, a 12 year old with a flair for the spotlight, especially singing on stage. During our latest sleepover with my friends from Sundance Springs, plus the addition of a mysterious friend, we go on another magical adventure where nothing is what it seems. My drama and dreams have turned my life upside down. I thought navigating middle school was tricky. Now I'm learning that being an adult is trifficult.

Copyright © 2021 by Mary Ann Jensen

Jensen Publishing
Cottonwood Heights, Utah

ISBN: 978-1-7345590-2-6

First Edition

10 9 8 7 6 5 4 3 2

Printed in the United States of America

This book was typeset in Archer, Million Notes and Frogurt.

This book is dedicated to
my best friend (and sister) Caroline,
my mom, my dad, my grandparents, and
all my totes 'mazing readers who returned for
more adventures in Sundance Springs.

English
GUIDEMAP

J-musement park

sement
rk
KET

TIC

EVENT
CODE:
A114
$82.9?

SEAT:
B127

11089
EBJ4?

110897
BBJ40

J-musement park

♪♫ Victor
Co

Livin' the Dream Soundtrack

Download the J-musement
Park app to get a free digital
map, PLUS a virtual scavenger
hunt through the park.

Chick-fil-t
chick-fil-A
sauce

INGREDIENTS:
MUSTARD, ONION,
CARAMAL (COLOR)
T, BBQ SAU-
SYRUP

eraser

My name is Victoria Hemmingsbird. I am 12 years old, in 6th grade, in French immersion, and I absolutely love to sing. I play the piano, and I study ballet. Since I'm an only child, my parents like to keep me busy. I am really good friends with Grace Roberts & Christy Pearl, but ever since our magical sleepover at Christy's house, Megan Fischer has been my absolute BEST friend.

I tease her that the only reason she moved here to Sundance Springs was to save my life! I was stranded in a bathroom! If she hadn't heard my cries for help, I'd probably still be there right now! OK, so I'm a little over dramatic. Now you know about me. If you thought that was an experience for the books . . . just you wait!!!

me, onstage SINGING!

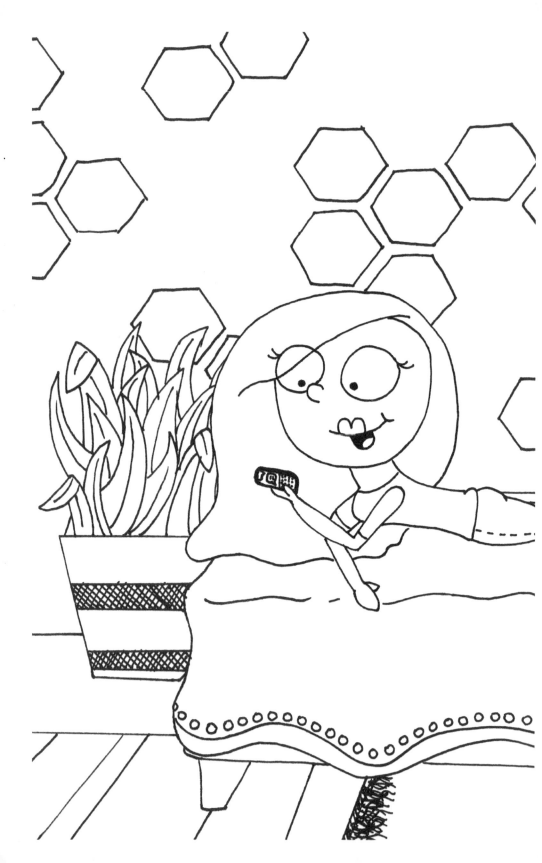

I get home from school and go up to my room as usual. Just as I sit down on my bed to get out my math homework, my phone dings. Grace Roberts just texted me! It reads:

Hi-ya V!
I'm hosting a sleepover this Fri, U R invited!
My house from 6pm to 12:30pm on Sat!
Text me if U can come!

Today, at school lunch, Grace suggested that we have another sleepover. The last one we had was an adventure. Christy Pearl woke up with lime green hair, half shaved off, Grace got blue fur, Nicolle Parker lost her violin, Sabrina Harrison became Brobee from Yo Gabba Gabba, and Megan Fischer converted to a mermaid whenever she touched water, all because of an insane game of Would You Rather. I seriously hope that Grace's family does *not* have any Ring cameras, and that we don't play a game of Would You Rather. But, Grace is a *phenomenal* friend, so I know that her sleepover will be just as incredible as she is.

I run downstairs and ask my mom if I can go. She says yes! So I text Grace back:

Sounds great! I'll be there! So x-cited!

* * * * *

I come home from school the next day, Tuesday.

Now I know that it's Tuesday so I don't need to start packing *yet*. But I do anyway. I learned from Megan that it's always good to pack for sleepovers *early*, so I place my red nightgown with the white lace around the bottom in my favorite silver sequined duffel bag. I also lay my favorite silver notebook, and silver mechanical pencils inside. I then put my red sleeping bag with silver accents, my toothbrush, and toothpaste, and an extra change of clothes inside my duffel.

At Christy's sleepover Megan had brought some jelly beans, which I thought was a *very* smart idea. You never know what can happen at a sleepover! I don't have *any* jelly beans, so I decide to put a package of baby fruit puffs inside my duffel. I eat them like cereal!

After I put the fruit puffs in my duffel, I stick in the CD that I put together. The songs in it are all my favorite! There's Taylor Swift, Carly Rae Jepsen, and songs from Barbie movies! People think that it's weird, but believe me! The songs are pretty incredible!

* * * * *

Friday morning I wake up extra early with excitement. Today is Grace's sleepover! I get up and get ready for school as fast as possible, even though I know that won't mean the sleepover will come *any* faster.

At school I can't focus at ALL! In math, I sit daydreaming in class about sleepovers.

"Victoria!" Mr. E. (our math teacher) yells in a stern voice, trying to snap me out of it. "What is the answer of 14 times 3?"

Janessa rolls her eyes.

"Uh... it's uh —" I say as Janessa cuts me off.

"It's 42!" she screams out as she looks back at me and smiles.

"Fabulous answer Janessa! You got it right! As for *you* Victoria, *you* need to finish *your* pop quiz!" he snaps at me.

Why is Mr. E. so nice to Janessa, but is so rude to me? It makes no sense! Maybe it's her curly, chocolate hair?

When school ends I grab my binder, and my backpack, out of my locker and rush outside to my mom's car. When we get home I put away my things, and then I sprint upstairs to my room, and check to make sure I have *everything* I need in my duffel bag. I check once, then twice, then three times, then four, then five, then I know that I am *definitely* ready for the sleepover.

Later around 5:30 pm I grab my duffel, and my mom drives me over to Megan's house. We pick her up and drive to Grace's house for the sleepover.

When Megan and I pull up onto Grace's driveway,

we grab our duffels and head up to her front door. Megan rings the doorbell, and Grace opens the door with a big, bright smile.

"Hi girls! I'm so glad you could come!!! You can go sit in the living room, I will take your bags.

"Thank you!" we say as we sit down.

A few minutes later, the doorbell rings again. It's Sabrina, Nicolle, and Christy. Grace leads us downstairs.

"My brother, Tanner will bring us down some food, so you can get situated," Grace says as her brother comes down balancing everyone's duffels and backpacks. Suddenly they all topple to the ground. All the girls and I rush over and grab our bags.

"Sorry girls," Tanner apologizes.

"It's okay," Grace says as the doorbell rings.

"I'll get it!" Grace's mom hollers.

"Who could *that* be?" Nicolle asks.

"What do you guys want to watch?" Tanner asks as he turns on the TV.

"Like I didn't know that she like invited like anyone else!" Sabrina says.

"Me neither," Christy adds.

"Star Wars?" Tanner asks.

"But if the doorbell rang then, someone else *probably* just arrived," Megan suggests.

"What about 'The Force Awakens'? That one is my *favorite!* Yeah, I'll turn that one on!" Tanner claims, talking to himself.

"Maybe it's Summer! She's in most of our classes at school!" I add as Grace's mom comes downstairs.

All of a sudden the Star Wars theme song comes on, and Janessa strides down the stairs. *Wait!* Janessa?

Questions fill my head. Why is Janessa here? Was she invited? Is Grace friends with her? But most importantly, why *Janessa?*

"Many of you may know Janessa. She goes to our school, and is in the same grade as us! Mr. E is her math teacher for sixth period. You may know her from that class, but if not, I want you to get to know her." Grace explains.

Janessa carries her duffel over to the couch. She sets it on the floor, then plops on the couch.

I walk over to Grace, who is telling Tanner that we are *NOT* watching Star Wars.

"Um . . . Grace, why did you invite *Janessa?*" I whisper, so Janessa won't hear.

"Hey, Vicky!" Tanner interrupts.

"It's Victoria, but whatever."

"Sorry, *Victoria*, do *you* want to watch Star Wars?"

"Uh, no, not especially."

"Dang it! I'll go ask Sabrina, and – !" Tanner says as he walks away.

"Sorry about *him*," Grace apologizes.

"No worries, but, why did your mom invite *Janessa?*" I ask.

"Oh, um... about that. My mom didn't invite her." she explains. "*I* did."

"But why *Janessa* of all people?"

"We kinda' forgot to thank her. I told you that Monday at school!"

"Sorry, I forgot. This sleepover has been the *only* thing on my mind for the past few days."

"It's alright. I've been doing *a lot* of preparations for tonight. I'm glad that I'm not the *only* one that's excited!" Grace says as she puts in a DVD.

Then the doorbell rings again!

"Who like could *that* be?" Sabrina asks in total confusion.

"That's the pizza!" Grace says.

"That makes *a lot* more sense!" Nicolle sighs.

"I'll go get it!" Tanner hollers as he rushes upstairs. When he comes back down he sets the pizza on the table.

"Thank you room service!" Grace says in a fancy British accent.

"Anything else I can get for you madame?" Tanner responds in a British accent.

"Some saucers and cups for tea."

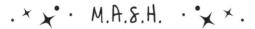

"Cheerio then, I'll be right back!"

When he comes back he brings some pink paper plates, along with some plastic cups that match. We eat our pizza while we watch Barbie Princess and the Popstar.

(Grace is a Barbie encyclopedia. She has watched *every* Barbie movie 100 times at least! Plus, she *loves* to point out Easter eggs, knows *every* character's voice, word to every song, *and* she owns *all* of the Barbie dolls that she can get her hands on! She's been telling us that we need to watch the movies. I've seen a few, but this sleepover is a *great* time to watch a movie together, so Barbie is a *fantastic* choice!)

When we finish the pizza, Grace's mom brings down some Rice Krispy treats with sprinkles in them. We scarf them down. Then, we take turns changing into our pajamas, in the bathroom.

We all sit down to play a game of Poison Dart Frog! It's where you sit in a circle, and one person is chosen to be the 'Poison Dart Frog'. Nobody knows who it is. This person has to make eye contact with another person in the circle, and stick out their tongue at them. If you get a tongue stuck out at you, you're 'dead'. So, you're out. It's really fun to act it out when you 'die'. I just fall on the floor and go 'bleh'. One person stands in the middle of the circle, and is the 'detective'. They look around and try to figure out who the poison dart frog is. They only get three guesses. If they guess right, the game is over, if they guess wrong, the game keeps going, until the frog has 'killed' everyone! Sounds like a really inappropriate game, but we learned it in gym class in elementary school, so I think it's fine!

"Do you guys want to play M.A.S.H.?" Janessa suggests. This is the first thing she's said all night. So, we're all pretty surprised.

"That sounds great!" Grace says.

"I've got a notebook!" Megan exclaims. So, we start discussing the rules.

If you've never played M.A.S.H., here are the rules. M.A.S.H. stands for Mansion, Apartment, Shack, and House. This game is to 'predict your future'. So, you pick three of your crushes, three cars you want, four numbers, three jobs, and three pets. Then you pick a number from one to ten. Let's say you picked the number four. You would start at the M in M.A.S.H., you would count M as one, A as two, S as three, and H as four. You would cross H out, then you would go to your crushes, then cars and so on. When one thing is left uncrossed in each category, then you 'read your future'. The letter in M.A.S.H. that's left uncrossed will be where you live, the crush that is left is the person who you will marry, the car that's left is the car you will have, the number that's left is how many children you will have, the job left will be your job, and the pet that's left is the pet you will have. Sometimes I do my celebrity crushes, and instead of cars I do submarines, helicopters, and airplanes, because I don't know all the fancy names of the cars. I mean, sometimes I just say 'red car' or 'blue car', because I'm not a car genius! It's a great game for sleepovers!

After everyone had their 'fortunes' read, these were the results:

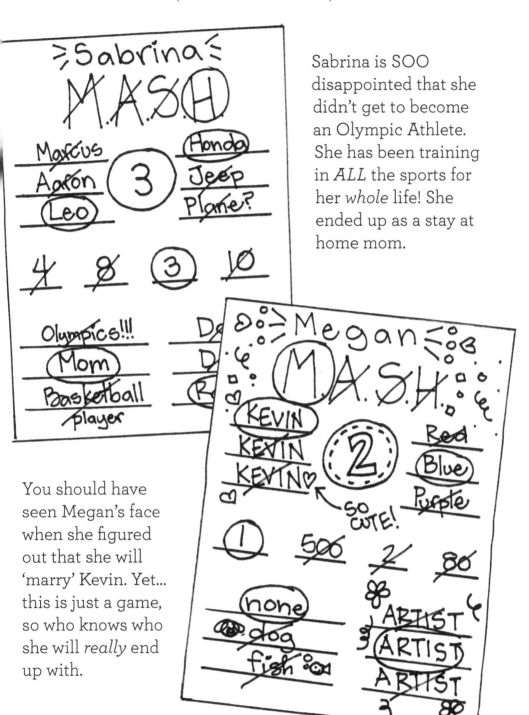

Sabrina is SOO disappointed that she didn't get to become an Olympic Athlete. She has been training in *ALL* the sports for her *whole* life! She ended up as a stay at home mom.

You should have seen Megan's face when she figured out that she will 'marry' Kevin. Yet... this is just a game, so who knows who she will *really* end up with.

So, Grace has always wanted to be a photographer, but for some reason she is ecstatic about her red car. She doesn't know what *kind* of car it is, just that it's *RED!*

Chick-fil-A! Janessa's job is at Chick-fil-A. That is seriously my *least* favorite restaurant *ever.* I mean you'd have to be *crazy* to work there!

Nicolle

M.A(S)H.

Flinn
♡ Aaron ♡
Allister

(7)

Minivan
Convertable
Jeep

4̶ 2̶ ① 3̶

My DREAM job!

singer
mom
actress

She loves to act.
She is currently
rehearsing for the
next school play,
'Cinderella.' So, I
think this is the
perfect job for her!

Christy

M(A)S(H)

Allister
Lazlo
Dylan

(3)

Ferrari
Limo
Convertable

1̶ 2̶ ⓪ 3̶

Cat
none
Dog

Model
Hair Stylist
Fashion
designer

Her dad is the mayor
of Sundance Springs,
so I was pretty sure
that she would end
up with 'mayor' as
her job! She is very
fashionable though,
so a fashion
designer is right up
her alley.

I'm happy with my results, all except for the cat. I mean, who wouldn't want to live in a mansion with *Allister Cookie!* He's such a hottie!

After the excitement of 'reading our futures', and gushing over who we will marry, we disperse and get out our sleeping bags.

It was a bit hard to go to sleep, because we practically talked all night.

Eventually we all fall asleep, but when we wake up...

...I wake up, and *oh my!* I sit up, and I'm *NOT* in Grace's basement! I'm in a *bed!* When I went to bed, I was in a sleeping bag on the *FLOOR!* Now I am on a *BED!* I look to my left, and there is a grown man laying next to me!!!

I'm *freaking* out!!! I tiptoe out of bed, because, I mean, if *you* saw a grown man laying next to you, that you don't know, in a place you don't know, you would want to get out ASAP! I turn the lamp on, just to see where I am. I notice a door! I run toward it. It's my ticket out of here!

Right before I reach the door, I trip. I look to see what I tripped on. It's my silver sequinned duffel bag! What is *it* doing here? I push it out of the way, and run out the door.

When I exit the bedroom, I hear crying. It's not the creepy grown man crying, I hear a *baby* crying! I follow the sound of the crying. I *need* to see what's going on! I hear it coming from the left side of the hallway, so I open the closest door on the left side of the hallway. I walk through the doorway, and feel cold tile under my feet. I turn on the lights. It's a bathroom! Not Grace's though. This one looks like a fancy shmancy bathroom that you would find in the luxury suite at an expensive hotel! It's *massive!* There is an *enormous* white bathtub, a *humongous* shower with octagon shaped shower tiles, and a large two sinked counter with a *huge* mirror above it! I look in the mirror and scream!!! I am clearly *NOT* twelve anymore, I look like I'm... um... *thirty!!!* But I also look like a supermodel! My hands are big, and perfectly and professionally manicured. My eyelashes are *insanely* long, and then... I look down.

"Whoa, *those* weren't there before!" I shriek.

All of a sudden the creepy grown man runs in.

"Is everything okay honeybuns?" he asks me. Honeybuns? Okay, what's going on here?

"Um, who are *you?*" I ask.

"Oh, silly."

"No, seriously, who are you?"

"I am your husband, Allister Cookie."

"What?"

"And you are my wife, Victoria Cookie."

"Okay, I'm dreaming!"

"No, honeybuns, you aren't dreaming."

"Fine! Pinch me!"

"No, no. I am *not* going to pinch you honeybuns!"

"Pinch me!" I insist. He follows as I say, "OW! Okay, this is all a misunderstanding!"

"No, it's not honeybuns."

"I'm twelve years old, we can't be married, someone is crying, and I DON'T LIVE HERE!!!"

"It's your night to feed Alice her bottle, honeybuns!"

"Okay, who is Alice, and I am *NOT* YOUR HONEYBUNS!!!" I scream.

"Alice is our daughter!"

"WHAT?!? I HAVE A *DAUGHTER!?!*" I scream. I'm *so* confused right now, I'm like thirty, I am married and have a daughter! I *literally* don't know what's going on right now!!!

* * * * *

I leave the bathroom, and follow the crying noise. I see an open door. I walk cautiously into the room, and see a crib. I walk over to it and see the cutest baby *EVER!!!* She has on little footy pajamas with smiley clouds and rainbows on them. I pick her up and see her cute little fingers and precious face. I run my finger across her soft cheek. Her crying quiets down. I carry her to the bedroom I woke up in, and grab the baby fruit puffs from my duffel.

I walk back to the baby's room and sit down on a rocking chair with Alice in my arms. I open the fruit puffs and put one in the baby's mouth. She instantly stops crying. After a few more fruit puffs, we both fall asleep.

* * * * *

In the morning I'm greeted by Allister, and a kiss! *EW!* Now, sure he was the cutest boy in all of sixth grade, but we're not in sixth grade anymore. So... I *sure* wasn't expecting a *kiss!!!*

We put baby Alice back in her crib. Then walk

downstairs.

"Honeybu– I mean, *Darling*. Did you have a good sleep?" Allister asks me.

"Yes, why?" I ask.

"Well, your concert is tonight! I don't want you to sleep through it!"

"What concert? Who's performing? Carly Rae Jepsen? Donny Osmond? *Taylor Swift?*"

"Oh, you silly. *Your* concert! *You* are performing!"

"Wait, *I* perform?!?"

"I hired a sitter for Alice. It'll be great!"

"Who's the sitter?"

"A girl named Sabrina! I already told you that!"

"You *did?*"

"You need to go practice your songs now!"

"What songs?"

"The songs you wrote!"

"*I* write songs?"

"Yes, and you have a concert tonight, so you should go review them!"

"Uh,"

"Christy will be over later."

"Wait! Christy Pearl!?!?!"

"No, Christy Harper. She is coming over to give you your costume. You really should be upstairs by now!"

"Is there sheet music?"

26

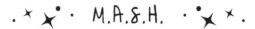

"I'm sure there is!"

"Where?"

"In the music room!"

"We have a *music room?*"

"Yes, now go practice!"

"Uh, yes. I'm on my way!"

*   *   *   *   *

I had to ask Allister where the music room was. He thinks that I'm losing my mind, because I don't know where anything is, or what I do, or who *he* is, or who *Alice* is, or even who *I* am! I personally don't know what's going on! He walks me through a hall, we go up an elevator. We then go through another hallway, and then we stop at a door. He gives me *another* kiss, *EW!!!* And then he walks off.

I open the door to find pearl white walls with gold designs on them, gold tiled floor, and lots, and *LOTS* of instruments! Flutes, trumpets, clarinets, oboes, saxophones, tubas galore, trumpets, French horns, violins, violas, cellos, basses, triangles, drums, recorders, bassoons, harps, timpani, contrabasses, an organ, guitars, piccolos, an English horn, a keyboard, keytars, accordions, and two pianos. One black, and one white.

In fifth grade, we were going to go to the symphony, and the teachers told us about all the different instruments. I was intrigued, so I went home and learned the names of as many of the instruments as I could. I watched videos to hear their sounds, and researched pictures to see what they looked like, but I would have never imagined to see them all in the same room! Well, besides at the symphony, but they didn't have a bassoon...or a guitar...or a keytar...or an accordion..or recorders...

I feel awkward, because in this *enormous* room full of an *insane* amount of instruments, I only know how to play one! The piano.

My *"husband"* says that I am *"performing my songs"* tonight, but since I don't know much in this *crazy* world, I don't even know what instrument he knows that I play! In Sundance Springs I played the piano. Since it's the only one I play, I decide to see what I've got.

I sit down on the white piano bench, and notice a piece of sheet music. I look at it. It's a song written in pencil, with a signature at the top. It reads *"by: Victoria Cookie"* I must have written this piece! I start to sight read it. Then, after a couple times, I start to sing with it.

* * * * *

I sing and play the music. I'm on cloud nine until suddenly someone walks in.

"That was *beautiful!*" she says.

"Thanks, you startled me!" I reply in shock.

"I'm Christy!"

"Ohmygosh! Christy *Pearl?* I didn't even recognize you! It's me, Victoria *Hemmingsbird!*"

"Oh wow! You look *so* different!"

"You do, too!"

"Why do we look this way? What's going on?"

"I have *no* idea!"

"Well I apparently am married to Dylan Harper, live in a house, have a Ferrari, have no children, no pets, and I'm a fashion designer!"

"That sounds amazing!"

"It really is!"

"Well, I'm married to Allister Cookie, have one child, live in an enormous mansion, and I'm a singer!" I say just as an orange tabby cat walks in. "And I have a cat, too, apparently!"

"I woke up in a dream!"

"A dream that I am having, too!" I say as my stomach grumbles.

"I thought I'd bring you over breakfast!" she says as she hands me a doughnut.

"Thank you!" I say as I take a huge bite.

"Oh, and you know me as Christy Pearl, but since I woke up, married to Dylan Harper, I'm now Christy Harper!"

"I like that!"

"Me, too!"

"It'll take some getting used to."

"And you are Victoria *Cookie!* That's an *amazing* last name!"

"Yes, it really is." I say as I realize that if *Christy* is here, what about the *others!* "Wait! Do you know what happened to the other girls?"

"No idea, but – " she starts as she runs outside. When she comes back, she is holding a big clothing protector. She unzips it. "*This* is for you!"

It's a *gorgeous* silver sequined dress with a red belt with black music notes on it. There are some quarter notes on the right corner of the dress, too. There is also some red fabric, floofing out of the bottom of the dress.

"It is *stunning!*" I exclaim "Where did you get it?"

"It was on my desk at home with a sticky note with your name and address on it!"

"I *love* it!" I say as the cat's tail tickles my leg.

Christy sets the dress down on the piano, and picks up the cat. "Hi!" she says as she looks at it's collar. "Hi Julius!" she says as she starts laughing hysterically. "That's *hilarious!* It's like what they have at Dairy Queen, you know, the Orange Julius drinks! And this cat's name is *Julius*, and it's *orange!*" Christy says as we burst into laughter.

Once Christy and I stop laughing, we walk into the room I woke up in. I bring the dress with me. Christy sits down on the bed, and I walk over to a closet door in the room. I open it, and inside it looks like Barbie's closet from Barbie Life in the Dreamhouse. I don't *love* that show, but I would watch it every once in a while. But I do *LOVE* this closet!

There are racks of clothes *everywhere!* There are shelves full of jewelry, and a whole wall of shoes!!! Forget about the rest of this house, I want to live in *this* closet! I try on the *gorgeous* dress that Christy brought me. I admire it in my mirror for a few minutes. Then, I twirl out of my closet.

"The dress looks amazing on you!" Christy exclaims.

"Thank you! I love it!" I say.

"Of course!" Christy responds.

After Christy and I had listed all of the adjectives that describe my dress, Allister walks in.

Christy leans over and whispers into my ear, "He was *definitely* cuter as a sixth grader."

"My thoughts exactly!" I whisper back.

Allister walks over to me and looks at the dress.

"Whoa Vicki! That dress is *gorgeous* on you! I told you that Christy Harper would be a great designer!" he states.

"It's actually Victoria, but thank you!" I correct.

"Thank you. It's an honor," Christy says.

"I've got to get to work, but I'll see you at the theater!" Allister finishes.

"Um, alright! Uh, thanks! See you later!" I say as he exits the room.

About twenty minutes later, we hear the doorbell ring. Christy and I jump. We rush downstairs to answer the door.

"Hi, I'm like apparently supposed to like babysit for um..." the girl at the door stammers as she checks her phone. "Um, like, Victoria Cookie?"

"Yes, that's me!" I exclaim.

"Like I'm Sabrina," the girl says.

"Are you Sabrina *Harrison?*" Christy asks.

"Like, yeah!"

"I kinda' thought it was you, because you said *'like'* like numerous times!" Christy laughs.

"Well, I'm Victoria Hemmingsbird!"

"And I'm Christy Pearl!"

"Oh like my gosh! That is like insane! I didn't like know you two were here! Have you seen anyone else that you like know?" Sabrina asks in excitement.

"No, we haven't. Have you?" Christy inquires.

"Nope, but I can't like believe you're here!" Sabrina exclaims. "I have like had a crazy morning! I woke up in a house with like, Leo Higgins. I have a Honda, three children, a pet rabbit, and like I'm a stay at home mom."

"All you need to know about me is that I'm a fashion designer, and am married to Dylan Harper!" Christy says.

"I'm married to Allister Cookie, and I'm a singer or something!" I explain.

"Well, that like explains the text message from Allister this morning explaining he like needed a sitter! I like ended up here, and can't believe you are here! Like I feel like I'm dreaming!" Sabrina exclaims.

"We feel the same way!" Christy and I add in unison.

"I have never liked the pinching thing, but..." Christy says as she sticks her arm out in front of me. "Pinch me!"

I pinch Christy timidly.

"Ow! *Definitely* not dreaming!" Christy says.

"Well –" I start just as the phone rings. "Is that *your* phone?" I ask the girls, because it is *definitely* not mine! Then I notice a phone on a table by the door. I pick it up and answer.

"Hello?" I ask.

"Hi! Is this Victoria Cookie?" the other person inquires.

"Uh, yes?" I respond questionably.

"Oh! Dahhhling, I just wanted to let you know that you have to be at the stage in an hour! We need to practice once more before the big show! It's gonna' be totes 'mazing!"

"Uh, where?"

"I'll text you the address *again!* Wear your costume! BYE!"

"Wait –" I say as she hangs up.

"Who was *that?*" she asks.

"I have *no* idea!" I say in total honesty.

"Well, who am I supposed to like babysit?" Sabrina inquires, changing the subject.

"Come upstairs and I'll show you!" I say as the girls follow me.

Once we get upstairs, we walk down a hallway to the baby's room. She is in her crib sleeping.

"She is *soooooooooooo* cute!" Sabrina and Christy whisper in unison.

"Her name is Alice," I tell them as I walk over to the rocking chair and pick up the fruit puffs. "She can eat these, and you can have some, too!"

"Like thanks! Bye!" Sabrina says as Christy and I leave the room and head downstairs.

*   *   *   *   *

Christy and I walk to the front door.

"If we need to get to the place where you'll be performing, let's go *now!*" Christy explains as we walk out the door.

I didn't get much time to look at the outside of the house, because the phone I had just answered a call on, dinged! I look at the text. It has the address of where I will be performing! The text reads:

> I've sent U this message about
> 5 times B4 but, whatev'!
> PLZ go 2 the j. Theatre on 10th Ave!
> C U soon!
> (PS! If U didn't hear me B4,
> wear your totes 'mazing costume!)

The garage door opens to reveal a *HUGE* garage, like, bigger than you could *ever* imagine! An *enormous* black limo pulls out!

The driver rolls down his window. "Hey Victoria! Where to today? You're going to do a practice concert, eh?" he asks.

"Um..." I say as I look at the message on the phone. "J. Theatre on 10th Avenue?"

"Hop in!" he says as the door slides open. He motions for us to get in. We do! Then the door slides behind us.

Christy and I sit down on the *huge* red seats inside the *enormous*, black, shiny limo! The seats are *super* comfortable.

The driver looks at us. "You gave me a copy of your songs in case you needed them before your concert or practice performance!" he explains.

"I did?" I ask questionably.

"Yup!" he adds as he hands me a sparkly silver folder with sheet music inside.

"Thank you!" I say as I take the folder.

In the limo there is candy in the cup holders, so I eat

a Hershey's Cookie's n' Cream bar! They are my *favorite!* Just as I take the first bite, I look outside. We're in the city! Suddenly I notice a *HUGE* sign with my face on it! *MY FACE* is on a huge sign in the city! The sign with my face on it reads:

VICTORIA COOKIE
performing LIVE at the j. Theatre!

I nudge Christy and show her the sign.

"No way! That's *awesome!!!*" Christy says.

"I can't believe that *I* am on a huge sign! I didn't know I was *that* famous!" I exclaim.

"Really? We pass by that sign *every* time we drive through town! I thought you had noticed it before!" the driver asks in confusion.

"Well, uh... maybe not!" I stammer.

When we finally get to the J. Theatre on 10th Avenue, the driver drops us off.

"Thank you, Mr. Driver!" I say.

"My pleasure!" he responds as he drives away.

Christy and I walk up to the entrance. It's *huge!* We're about a half an hour early, so we decide to look around. There are *enormous* golden chandeliers in the lobby, red velvety carpet, and white satin chairs. How can I perform *here?* This place should be for *royalty*, not a town girl who got transported here this morning who has absolutely *no* idea what's going on! That's the *total* opposite of royalty!

Christy and I decide to check out the auditorium. We

enter the large doors, and see some people on the stage. There's one girl who starts to sing. Christy and I sit on some chairs by the back of the auditorium, because they're the closest, and all the rest are full.

The girl singing looks vaguely familiar! I pull out my phone, which I know I shouldn't do during a show, but I go to my camera, and zoom in on her face. I snap a picture and look at it.

"Who is *that?*" I ask as I show the picture to Christy.

"She looks familiar," Christy says as she knits her eyebrows together in confusion.

"But where would we know her from?"

* * * * *

After the bows, and the auditorium empties, Christy and I walk out. We notice a girl exit from the 'Cast Only' door.

Christy and I walk over to her.

"Hi!" I say.

"Did you like the performance?" she asks.

"Yes, but, I'm Victoria, and this is Christy!" I interrupt.

"Wait! Victoria *Hemmingsbird?*" she asks.

I nod.

"And Christy *Pearl?*"

Christy nods.

"I... I'm Nicolle Parker!" she exclaims.

"Okay, okay, *you're* Victoria, and *you're* Christy? This is *crazy!!!* Did you wake up here, too? I thought I was dreaming! I woke up, living in a shack. I know, a shack!?! Yes, I woke up in a shack, with Aaron Ducet, have one child, along with a pet turtle, a Jeep, and I'm apparently an actress!" she explains.

"Nicolle, I can't believe it's you!!!" Christy and I say as we give her a big hug.

She's not in her costume anymore, she is now wearing a maroon colored t-shirt, a navy blue belt, and denim capris.

"You were *amazing!*" I exclaim.

"Thank you! It was kind of all improv since I woke up this morning and I was told I had to perform. I didn't even get a *glimpse* of the script!" she explains.

"Literally *amazing!*" Christy and I say in unison.

"No, your dress is *literally amazing!*" Nicolle says.

"Thank you, Christy made it!" I tell her.

"Well, not *really*, I woke up and found it on my desk.

There was a sticky note on it with Victoria's name on it. So, I *really* didn't make it," Christy explains.

"Who cares! It's *amazing!*" Nicolle says as a girl rushes over to us. She has short red hair in a bob, she has black glasses with oversized lenses, a black and white polka dotted t-shirt, black capris, and tall red high heels. She gives me a hug, which is weird because I don't know her.

"Victoria! Darling! You look *stunning!*" she says. How does she know my name?

"Uh-" I stutter.

"Come on Victoria, let's go!" she says.

"Uh, who are you?" I ask.

"Silly, silly come on!" she says as she grabs my arm and drags me out of the theater lobby. Christy and Nicolle follow me, but the crazy lady pulls me through a "Cast Only" doorway, and shuts the door before my friends can get in.

Christy and Nicolle bang on the door.

"Sit down," the crazy lady says as she points to a red salon chair.

Reluctantly, I sit down.

"Fans are so, *so* demanding!"

"Actually those aren't *just* fans, they're my *best* friends!" I correct.

"Oh! I apologize! *That* explains it!" she says as she opens the door and lets them in. "You two sit there!" she says as she points to a daybed with red cushions and black and white checkered pillows on it. She then walks over to a cupboard and grabs some hair supplies. She brushes through my hair.

Then she plugs in a curling iron and curls my hair. I have *long* hair, so the ringlets are long. After it's all curled she sprays some extra hold hairspray, and some glitter spray in my hair. I hop out of the chair and she leads me to an *enormous* mirror.

"Thank you!" I exclaim.

"Oh, I'm not finished!" she responds as she pulls open the mirror like it's a door. Inside, there is makeup *galore!* She pulls a stool out of the mirror/closet thing, and I sit. She grabs powders, and creams, blushes, glosses, glitters, and more stuff that I can't name. She puts it all on my face. She spins around the stool when she's done.

"*Wow!*" I exclaim as I see my face. I don't even recognize it at first!

"Finished!" she says.

"Are you for reals!?!" I ask, stunned. I'm *literally* speechless. I look *outstanding!!!* "I can't believe this!!! Thank you!!!"

"I'm *so* glad!"

All of a sudden a girl with pitch black hair in a messy bun rushes in. She comes straight over to me and the girl who did my makeup. This new lady is wearing a hot magenta top, with a bright coral jacket, and turquoise capris. She's also wearing cute little earrings with rainbow colored tassels, and has a bright yellow backpack slung over one shoulder.

"O, M, Goodness!!! Vicki!!!" she exclaims as she gives me the tightest hug *ever!* You know how in movies when someone's really excited to see someone, and so they give them a *humongous* hug, and then they say 'I can't breathe', well, that's what this is!

"Huh?" I say as I try to squeeze out of the hug.

"I am *sooooooooooooo* excited that you're here!!! You look totes 'mazing!"

"Who are you?"

"Are you *serious?* You can't remember who *I* am? I'm your *manager, Liza!!!* I called and texted you earlier!!! I was worried you would get lost and wouldn't be able to make it here in time for a practice run of the concert! But you are here, and you made it and that's totes 'mazing!!!" she babbles.

"Totes 'mazing?" I ask as a girl in black, with a headset on, peeks in.

"You're on in ten!" she says.

"Who's 'on in ten?'" I ask.

"*YOU!!!*" she shouts.

* * * * *

Liza and I walk out into the lobby. We walk over to the concession stand. Liza marches behind the desk, and pulls out a silver stick, that kind of looks like a fairy godmother's magic wand.

"What's that?" I ask her.

"It's the building transformation wand, *duh!*" she says.

"Um, okay? What does it do?" I ask.

"It does what it sounds like it does, *duh!*"

"It transforms buildings?"

"Yeah! Isn't that like totes 'mazing?!?"

"Uh huh, totes 'mazing?"

"Okay!" Liza says as she points the 'building transformer' to the chandelier. She flicks her wrist, and all of a sudden '*POOF!*' the building that we are in, transforms.

The gorgeous red velvety carpet floor is now gray concrete. *Bleh.* The enormous golden chandeliers are now silver pendant lights. *Ew!* And the white satin chairs are now dark purple bean bag chairs. *YUCK!*

"Um, this doesn't go with the color scheme! That's so not totes 'mazing!" Liza says as she flicks the wand again. The awful gray concrete is still awful gray concrete, but there is a red carpet leading to the auditorium doors. The ugly silver pendant lights are still ugly silver pendant lights, but on the ceiling and walls, there are huge red and silver star decals, along with large black music note decals. And the gross dark purple bean bag chairs are now red satin couches. *PHEW!* "Now it goes with our color scheme!" Liza says proudly. "Doesn't it look totes 'mazing!?!"

"Yes! It does!" I say in awe.

"Oh! We better get back to the stage to practice!!! You'll be totes 'mazing!!!"

"Will you just stop it with the *'totes 'mazing'*?"

"If I did, that would totes *not* be totes 'mazing!"

"*Ugh!*" I groan as we walk back to the 'Cast Only' door.

We re-enter the 'Cast Only' room. Liza leads me to a door with a giant marquee star on it. She looks at me in a way that makes me think that I have lobsters crawling out of my ears!

"Why are you looking at me like that?" I ask.

"You're missing something!" Liza replies as she rummages through her backpack.

"What am I missing?"

"Aha!" she says as she pulls a hairspray bottle out of her backpack. She sprays an insane amount in my hair.

"I was missing *hairspray?*"

"Wait!" she screams as she freezes and drops the hairspray can on the floor. She starts pulling things out of her bag and then tossing them behind her. She pulls out a tube of orange lip gloss, "No," she says as she tosses it behind her. She pulls out a Hello Kitty Paradise Fun and Games VHS. "No," she says as she tosses that behind her. She then pulls out a pink toaster. Yes! That's what I said. *A PINK TOASTER!* "Nope!" she says as she tosses that behind her, too!

"Why did you just fling a toaster behind you?!?"

"Cuz' it's not what I'm lookin' for!"

"But –" I start as she pulls out a bottle of glitter spray.

"Aha!" she says as she sprays a *psychotic* amount in my hair, and then all over my body! "Take a deep breath and go out there! You can do this!"

"Thank you!" I say as I gather my confidence. Liza opens the door with the huge marquee star on it and nudges me.

"This is just a practice run, the real concert is tonight, so get out there and show us what you've got! You've *totally* got this!"

"I've *totally* got this!"

"You'll be totes 'mazing!"

I roll my eyes.

"You got this!"

"I got this!"

"That's the spirit!" Liza says as she pushes me through the doorway.

As I walk through the doorway I see that the whole auditorium has changed! When Christy and I came in to see Nicolle, there were *millions* of seats. Now the floor is just plain old concrete, but it's *flat!* The stage is different, too! It's not just a normal rectangular stage, it's ovally, and there is a runway part connecting to it that goes out into the audience! It looks like Hannah Montana could perform here!

I stand in the middle of the oval stage, where there is a red and silver bedazzled microphone stand, with a matching microphone inside! There is hardly anybody in the audience, but Liza did tell me that this was just a practice concert, so what am I to expect?

I pick up the microphone, and then look over at Liza, who's standing in the doorway that I walked through. She mouths something to me. I look at her with confusion. She mouths it again. I shrug my shoulders to tell her that I don't know what she's saying. She picks up a piece of poster board and a Sharpie, and writes:

Say 'hello' to the audience, and introduce your most popular song!

So, I take the microphone and think of the Barbie movie, Barbie Princess and the Popstar. (We watched it with Grace at the sleepover.) In it, there's a popstar named Kiera, and she performs on stage. Since I've watched this movie a *gazillion* times, you could say I have it memorized! I try to remember what Kiera said before she performed. I think she said something like, 'Hey, Maribella! I'd like to dedicate this next song to my friends *blank* and *blank*. They taught me *blank!* I'd also like to dedicate this song to my best friend and sister, Tori!' I turn on the microphone and say *my own take* on what Kiera said to introduce the songs.

"Hey!" I say as I try to think of the name of the town I'm in. I can't think of it! "Hello, *town?!?*" I say feeling stupid. "I will be singing... *a song* now!" I say feeling like a fake, because I can't even think of the title of *my own* song!

My confidence drains as the song turns on. First, I don't know the name of the town, second, I can't remember the name of my own song, and third, I miss my queue, that's theatre language, but it really means, when the song got to the part that I am supposed to start singing at, I didn't start singing. I'm a counterfeit! I run off stage. The few people in the audience gasp. I go back to the 'Cast Only' room. Sabrina arrived!!!

I give her a huge hug. "Thank you *so* much for coming, and bringing my duffel!" I exclaim.

"What are you doing? This is *not* totes 'mazing!!! The show *must* go on!!!" Liza shouts.

I grab my duffel and pull out the remix CD that I put together myself. "It *will!*" I say proudly as I shove the CD into Liza's hands. "Song number fourteen."

"What?" Liza says in downright confusion.

"The show *will* go on!" I say as I walk back on to the

stage with the most confidence I've ever had in my *entire* life!

* * * * *

I walk back onstage. The few people in the audience, (which by now I know are workers at this theatre, I can tell by their uniforms) cheer and go crazy! When the CD turns on, it's 'Perfect Day' from Barbie Princess and the Popstar! I sing:

Sun's up, it's a little after twelve
make breakfast for myself

Leave the work for someone else
people say, they say that it's just a phase

They tell me to act my age
well I am!

On this perfect day
nothing's standing in my way

On this perfect day
where nothing can go wrong

It's the perfect day
tomorrow's gonna come too soon

I could stay forever as I am
On this perfect day!

When I finish singing the song, the few people in the audience cheer louder than *ever* before!

I look over through the doorway, and see Christy, Nicolle, Sabrina, Liza, and the girl that did my *astonishing* makeup and hair. They're all clapping and cheering for me, too!

The next song turns on, and this one is a song by Carly Rae Jepsen. I feel a little self conscious, because these aren't *my* songs, but this is *my* concert. I sing the song. This is just a *practice* anyway!

I jump around the stage and do ballet moves that I know by heart. Sadly, being an adult isn't at all that it's made up to be. I can't move my body the way I could when I was *"younger."* Yikes!

I sing a bunch more songs after that. I feel *incredible!* I can just sing my heart out, and nobody cares if I get the lyrics wrong! I'm not saying that my shower head is judgy, but this is the best feeling; to perform in front of *real* people! They clap and cheer! My shower head can't do *either* of those things!

After I sing fifteen or so songs, my throat hurts like *never* before. I decide that I should probably stop singing *now*, before I lose my voice!

"Thank you all for coming! It was such a pleasure to sing for all of you! You were an amazing audience!!!" I say into the microphone. So badly I want to do a mic drop! I have heard about them and have seen them in movies, so I drop the mic. It makes a 'boom, plof' and 'screech' as it hits the ground. But when I drop it, I feel like the coolest person in the *whole entire* world! Who cares that I can't do ballet! I'm the queen of the world!

Just before I can walk off of the stage and back to my friends in the 'Cast Only' room, a girl with short brown hair runs up to the stage. She's wearing an aqua t-shirt with a silver jacket overtop, she's also wearing some darling denim capris, a silver belt, silver sneakers, an aqua bow in her hair, a camera around her neck, and a coral backpack slung over one shoulder.

"Hi!" she says.

"Hello?" I respond.

"You're Victoria Hemmingsbird, right?" she asks.

I look at her in confusion. Everyone here knows me as Victoria Cookie, considering the huge sign I saw on the drive here! Wait! Everyone here knows me as Victoria Cookie, *except* for my *friends!* "Okay, hold on, how do you know me as Victoria *Hemmingsbird?*" I ask.

"Well," the girl says as she takes the backpack off her shoulder. She unzips it, and pulls out posters, CDs, t-shirts, a backpack, note books, pillows, and blankets with me, Victoria Cookie, on them! "On the CD cases, pillows, blankets, and t-shirts, et cetera, it says, Victoria Cookie. When I heard you sing today you sounded familiar. You sounded like Victoria Hemmingsbird, from when we used to use Christy's karaoke machine!"

"What?"

"I went on a search for merchandise once I saw the huge 'Victoria Cookie' sign from the freeway!" she says as she smiles intently. She pulls a box out from her backpack. She shows it to me. There's a Barbie doll inside! The labels on the front of the box say: 'Victoria Cookie' "They even make a Barbie doll of you!!!" the girl says excitedly. "This is my absolute *favorite* piece of merchandise!!!"

"You're definitely a superfan!" I say. "Did you just want to come up to get my autograph? I'll go grab a pen, I'll sign the Barbie box!'"

"No, I'm not a superfan! I'm *Grace!*" I stop and stare. Not at the incredible Barbie doll, I stare at Grace.

"Grace *Roberts!?!*"

"Yes, Grace *Roberts!!!*" she responds as Christy, Nicolle, and Sabrina run over.

"*GRACE?!?*" they squeal in unison.

"I woke up as a fashion designer, Nicolle woke up as an actress, and as you can tell, Victoria woke up as an incredible singer!" Christy exclaims.

"What did *you* wake up as?" Grace asks Sabrina.

"I just woke up as like a stay at home mom," Sabrina explains.

"I woke up with Flinn Cosman, no pets or kids. But I *am* a photographer and have a *red car!*" Grace explains as she holds up her camera. "But, I'm *so* happy that I found you girls!" she says as we do a group hug. She parts away quickly. "Wait! Where's Megan?!?"

"*Megan?*" Nicolle asks.

"Yes! Where's Megan?" Christy inquires.

"Have any of you seen Megan?" I ask.

We all shake our heads.

"Oh no! What if Megan didn't wake up here with us!?!" Grace screams as Liza walks over to us.

"Y'all didn't just *wake up* here! What *are* you talking about?" Liza asks.

"Okay Liza, here's the thing, yesterday night all of us were at Grace's house for a sleepover. We were all just kids. We woke up here, as adults." I explain.

"What did you *do* at the sleepover?" Liza asks unbelievingly.

"Well, we played poison dart frog," Grace explains.

"*Then* what?" Liza laughs.

"Then M.A.S.H.!" Christy continues.

"That's it!" I exclaim.

"What's *it?*" Liza asks.

"*M.A.S.H.!* We played M.A.S.H. and then woke up *in* our M.A.S.H.es!" I explain.

"You're all *very* funny!" Liza says sarcastically.

"I woke up with my duffel! Did any of you?" I ask.

They all nod their heads.

"Who has the notebook where we wrote our M.A.S.H.es in, so we can compare our answers with what we woke up with?" Christy asks.

"*Megan!*" Grace exclaims. "Megan has the notebook!"

"Where is she?" Nicolle asks.

"Like, no idea!" Sabrina blurts as Liza's stomach rumbles.

"Forget about your *'crazy wake up thing'* and I'll take you out for some totes 'mazing food!" Liza explains. "Vicky, can we take your limo?"

"You have a limo?" Sabrina, Grace, and Nicolle ask in unison.

"Yes! Let's go!" I say as we exit the stage and head to the parking lot.

Liza, Christy, Grace, Sabrina, Nicolle, the girl who did my hair and makeup, and I rush over to the limo, waiting at the curb.

The front window goes down. "Yo, Superstar! Where to?" the driver asks. Liza pulls a paper and pen out of her pocket. She writes something down and shows it to the driver. He laughs. "Sounds good!" he says to Liza. "Y'all can hop in!" he says as the door slides open.

The seven of us get in.

"This is *a lot* squishier than earlier!" Christy exclaims.

"Yes, it really is!" I respond.

We drive around for about fifteen minutes. When we finally stop, the driver looks at us.

"Y'all can get out now, we're here!" he says as the door slides open.

We get out and see Chick-fil-A.

"You're *kidding* me! *Chick-fil-A?*" I say in utter disappointment. I don't like Chick-fil-A.

"Y'all can get out now! We're here to get some totes 'mazing food!" Liza says as we squeeze out of the limo.

Sabrina runs ahead. "It's like not every day you get to eat at Chick-fil-A! I'm like getting a Spicy Chicken Deluxe Sandwich Combo!" she announces as she rushes inside.

"Y'all order! I'll pay!" Liza explains as we walk inside and get in line.

"Excuse me?" the lady at the counter says in a snotty way as she chomps loudly on a piece of gum when it's my turn to order.

"Oh!" I say as I get over the fact that I'm about to eat at my *least* favorite restaurant.

"What can I get you?"

"Oh, um... I'll have the –"

"Pick up the pace! I should be on my lunch break now!" she says curtly.

"Okay, let's see I'll have the –"

"Oh! My! Gosh! *You're* Victoria Cookie!!!" she screams as her gum flies out of her mouth, and lands on the middle of the cash register's screen.

"Yes, and I –"

"Can I get your autograph!?!"

"Uh, sure?"

"I'm your *biggest* fan! I started a fan club with all my friends!"

"That's... nice, I guess –"

"No, I'm not your *biggest* fan, I am your biggest, *biggest* fan!"

"Oookay?"

"No, no wait! I am your biggest, biggest, *BIGGEST* fan!"

"You know, um, I'd like to order some food –"

"You know, I am your biggest, biggest –"

"Biggest hugest, whatever! I would like a Coke, chicken bites, and a side of waffle fries, please!" I interrupt.

"Um, excuse me! You're holding up the line! Just order already!" the lady standing behind me in line, shouts disturbingly loud in my ear.

"*Who cares!* This is *Victoria Cookie!* Hear me? *VICTORIA COOKIE!*" the cash register lady states. "You don't wanna mess with this popstar, nuh uh!"

"Well, I'm hungry, so let me order!" the lady behind me says.

"I'd say you're *hangry!*" the cash register lady laughs.

"You wanna see me *angry?*"

"Um, I can see that you are angry *now!*"

"*Yeah!* So let *me* order!" the lady behind me announces as Liza pulls me out of the line.

"*Thank you,* Liza!" I exhale. "That was *totes 'mazing!*"

"'O' course! Meet you at the table. I'll share my waff' fries with ya,'" Liza says.

"Thanks!" I sigh as I walk over to the counter where they have straws and sauces and what not! I grab some Chick-fil-A Barbecue sauce!

On my way back to the table I bump into a cow! Not an *actual* cow, but a person *dressed* in a Chick-fil-A cow costume. "Sorry!" I say to the cow. Okay, that sounded really weird. However, when I said 'sorry' to the cow, I thought it rolled it's eyes at me. Well, the person inside the costume. Is this making any sense? This probably doesn't make any sense. This is all just very, *very* weird!

I walk over to the table that Liza saved for me and my friends, and try to ignore the cow eyeing my every move.

Liza comes over to the table with a table tent that has the number 10 written on it. She sits down with us, and sets some drink cups down on the table.

"Does anyone remember anything about Megan's M.A.S.H.?" I ask, because I can't get my mind off of the cow, so I try to change the subject.

"You really believe in this weird, 'I-went-to-bed-as-a-six-year-old-and-woke-up-as-a-thirty-five-year-old' nonsense?" Liza asks as she laughs hysterically.

"Uh, like we *definitely* weren't *six!*" Sabrina defends.

"Since we've all recognized each other, I'm *sure* we could recognize her!" Grace says enthusiastically.

"If I were Megan, where would I be?" Nicolle asks.

"Wait! What are some of Megan's favorite things?" Christy asks. "If we were to think of some of the things she likes, maybe we could find her!"

"She loves jelly beans, jellyfish, mermaids, the color violet –" I start listing "– and art! She loves art!!!"

I run outside to the limo and tap on the window.

The driver rolls down his window. "Hey, Superstar! What do ya' need?" the driver asks.

"You know the city soooooooooooooo much better than me and my friends, so will you take me to all the art places in town?" I ask. "Please?"

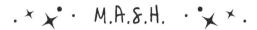

"Sure! Hop in!" he says as the door slides open.

I jump in the limo, and we're off.

*   *   *   *   *

We stop outside of a small building with a large sign that reads: 'DO sm'ART!'. I get out of the limo and walk inside. A girl with long blonde hair is sitting at a table, with paper covering it. There are buckets full of crayons, glue, markers, scissors, colored pencils, washi tape, normal clear tape, pencils, pens, glitter glue, paints, paint brushes, Sharpies, pastels, chalks, erasers, and gel pens. The buckets full of art supplies, are hung up on one of the walls. On one of the other walls, there's a huge bulletin board with art collaged onto it. The other two walls have splatters of paint splashed in every color imagined. There's ribbon strung across the ceiling, with little paper clips holding art, so there is art everywhere you look. Megan would *love* this place.

I walk up to the lady with long blonde hair.

"Hello! Would you like to make sm'ART?" she asks. "Our next class starts in about ten minutes! We will be making 3D flowers!"

"Do you know anyone named Megan?" I ask.

"No, I don't sorry about that!" she responds.

A family enters the building. They gasp loudly.

"Mommy!" their littlest daughter says excitedly as she points at me. "It's the girl on the big sign!"

Their teenage daughter rushes up to me clutching her phone tightly. "OHMYGOSH! YOU'RE VICTORIA COOKIE!!!" she screams as she starts taking selfies with me.

A couple more families walk in. All of their teenage daughters rush up to me and take selfies and start posting them on social media.

"I TOTALLY CAN'T BELIEVE *YOU'RE* HERE!!!" they all scream.

I can't stand their screaming, so I rush out the door.

The girls chase me.

I bang on the driver's window. The door to the limo slides open. I get in as fast as I can and slam the door behind me.

"Go, go, go!!!" I scream as we speed off.

"*That* didn't go as planned," the driver says. "Still want me to take you to all the art places in town?"

"I *have* to find Megan!" I say.

We stop in front of another building. This one is a store called 'J's Art Palace'.

"Thank you!" I tell the driver as I get out of the limo. "I'll be right back!"

"You betcha'" he responds. I walk into the store. There's art stuff everywhere. It reminds me of Michaels or JoAnn, except it's *a lot* bigger, and more colorful. I walk up and down each of the aisles looking for Megan.

As I walk down one of the aisles, I see a huge display of washi tape. I browse through the bins of washi tape. I find a roll with smiling clouds on it. It's only a dollar! How can I resist? I walk down the rest of the aisles with the tape in my hand. After the last aisle, I walk through all of them *again*, just to check for Megan. It's good to double check. After I look through all of them for a second time, I go to check out.

"Did you find wh– *OH WOW!* You're *Victoria Cookie!!!*" the lady exclaims.

"Yes I am," I say as I reach down to where a pocket would be on my dress. There's no pocket! "Dang it! I don't have any money with me!" I mumble under my breath.

"Keep the tape," the lady says. "You're *famous!* You *deserve* the tape! Do you need any more? Would you like me to put it in a bag? Can I take a selfie with –"

"Thank you!" I interrupt as I grab the tape and rush outside before anyone else notices me. This fan crazy thing is *really* getting crazy!

Of course when I get outside, people see me and chase me. I jump into the limo.

"So, how'd it go?" the driver asks me.

"No Megan; I *did* get some free tape though!" I exclaim.

"Why don't we try *one* more art place?"

"That sounds great!" I say as we drive off.

We pull up in front of a building with a sign that reads 'J's P-ART-Y!' Suddenly I get a text from Christy.

Christy: Hey V! R U OK? Where R U? We thought U went 2 the bathroom, but U have been gone 4 over an hour! WHERE R U!?!

Me: So sry! I'm looking 4 Megan.

I'm in the limo @ an art place called 'J's P-ART-Y'! Hope I find her soon!

Christy: Me 2! Good luck!

Me: C U L8R, hopefully w/ Megan!

Christy: Yes, hopefully!

I set the phone down on the seat and get out of the limo. Whoa! J's P-ART-Y is about as big as Lowe's! How am I *ever* going to find her here!?!

I walk in and to the right I see eight colorful doors with little whiteboards on them. The whiteboards read, 'Reserved for...'. To my left I see a huge, and colorful art warehouse! There are aisles, and aisles, and aisles for miles. There is a *full aisle* for scissors, *three full aisles* for paper, *eight full aisles* for stickers, and they even have a *full aisle* for washi tape!

A worker lady walks up to me. "Would you like to make a reservation?" she asks.

"Uh, no, but do you happen to know a girl named Megan?" I ask.

"No, I don't but, wait! Are you Vi–"

"Yes I am!" I interrupt as I pick up the nearest piece of paper and a pen and autograph it. "Here!" I say as I shove the paper into her hands.

"Oh my gosh!!!" she says as she about faints.

I can't stand to have another fan crazy breakout 'thing', so I rush back out to the limo, without even investigating the warehouse to find Megan.

When I get back to the limo, my phone dings.

Liza: Christy told me U were looking 4 your friend. That's great, but we have a meeting L8R, I mean, now! So, as soon as u get this message, come back 2 Chick-fil-A!

Me: Sounds good! I'm OMW!

"Sorry Mr. Driver, I feel so bad I don't know your name. What is it?" I ask the driver.

"It's alright! You can call me J." he responds.

"J?"

"Yes, J."

"Okay! Cool! J, will you take me back to Chick-fil-A? My friends are waiting!"

"Alrighty! Let's go!" he says as we pull out of the parking lot of J's P-ART-Y.

Once we get back to Chick-fil-A, I rush inside. I bonk into the cow on my way to the table. What am I going to do! I'll have *nightmares* of Chick-fil-A cows!

"Victoria! *There* you are!" the girls exclaim. "What *were* you doing? Where *were* you?" they all ask in a relieved tone.

"I was looking for Megan, but Liza messaged me to say that we have a meeting to go to!" I explain.

"That's right! We are gonna' be late! That wouldn't be totes 'mazing would it?" Liza says frantically "Go! We've got to get to the limo!"

"Like come on!" Sabrina says as she races us outside. Everything is a competition for her! Literally *everything!*

We get in the limo and Grace hands me a bag with my chicken bites and waffle fries.

"I thought you might be hungry!" she says.

"Thank you! I really *am* hungry! Sorry I ran off like that!" I apologize.

"No biggie! I understand that you want to find Megan. I really want to find her, too! She's such a great friend, so we've got to be great friends in return!" Grace says. She has a point.

"Thanks again for the food, Grace!" I say with a mouth full of waffle fries.

We all burst into laughter.

"It's like you're kids in an adult's body!" Liza says as she gets into the limo.

"We *are!*" Nicolle laughs.

Once we stop I look out the window.

"Here's your stop!" J says as Liza and I get out of the limo. "The rest of ya' can stay in the limo. I'll take ya' somewhere!"

We've stopped in front of an *extremely* tall building. On the front of the building, there's a *huge* sign that reads: 'J's Music House'. I follow Liza inside.

We get into an elevator. Liza presses a button. When the doors open, I see a modern looking octagon tiled wall, with a huge silver number thirty on it. There's a modern aqua colored couch with white pillows on it. A man with a cheetah print suit, black tie, purple shoes, and sunglasses on is sitting on the couch. He stands up right as we exit the elevator.

"Victoria, my star!" he exclaims as he gives me a huge hug. "Sorry for the late notice about the meeting! How was the concert?" he asks curtly.

"It was so much fun! When I walked out on stage I felt like I was dreaming –" I start as the man cuts me off.

"Victoria!" he snaps. "It was broadcasted on *every* station! You were supposed to sing *your* songs, not some stupid songs from the *fiftys!* YOU WERE *AWFUL!!!*" he says.

"No she wasn't! I told her that the show must go on, and

it *did!* She found a way! Her songs were impressive! And totally totes 'mazing!" Liza defends.

"Oh don't even make me think about her dancing! She looked like a dying bird!"

"Wait! It was broadcasted on *every* station? I thought you said this was a *practice* concert!" I ask in confusion.

"Yeah, I just said that! It was actually a broadcasted concert!" the man says bluntly.

"But –" I start as my phone rings. Grace is calling! "Sorry! I have to take this!" I say as I click the answer button.

The man and Liza keep bickering.

"MEGAN!" Grace says excitedly.

"Wait, *what!?!*" I ask in confusion.

"WE FOUND MEGAN!!!"

"Where are you?!?"

"We are at the J-musement Park!"

"Okay! I'm on my way!" I say as I get in the elevator. Liza and the man run toward the elevator, but the doors shut before they can reach me.

*   *   *   *   *

I exit the building and jet to the nearest car. Allister is inside.

"Take me to the J-musement Park!" I demand.

"I thought you had a meeting!" Allister responds.

"My friends are more important than the meeting!" I say as I get into the car.

70

"Whatever you say, honeybuns," Allister says as we speed off.

* * * * *

Once we enter the J-musement Park's parking lot, I sprint to the ticket booth. There is a large sign that reads: "Tickets, kids under four, free! Four to eight, $39.99. Nine to twelve, $44.99. Thirteen to sixty four, $49.99. Senior citizens sixty five and up, $42.99. One ticket lasts for one day, and one day only!"

The lady in the ticket booth is sitting on a stool, checking her social media.

"One ticket please!" I say.

No response.

I quickly read her name badge. "I'd like a ticket, Nancy," I say as I raise my voice. Then it hits me, I don't have any money to buy a ticket! UGH! What am I going to do?

I start to walk away as I sing 'Perfect Day' sadly under my breath.

"*WAIT!*" I hear.

I look around. I hear it again. I see a girl running towards me. Oh no! Here we go *again!* I expect fans with cameras, and papers for autographing, but no. It's a girl wearing a uniform with the J-musement Park logo on it! Once she catches up to me, she says.

"*Please* don't leave! What do you want? The girl at the other booth has been on her phone *all* day!" she explains.

"Well, I came here for a ticket to get into the park," I say, surprised that she isn't going fan/paparazzi crazy! "Guess I can't get in," I tell the worker.

"Why?" she asks.

"I don't have any money with me!"

"What are you talking about? You're *Victoria Cookie*, the amazingly fantastic singing star!!! You're *famous!!!* You get in for *free!!!*"

"*What?*"

"Did you *not* see the sign?"

"I *did* see the sign!"

"Look a little closer!" she suggests as she points to the sign. Suddenly I see that under where it says 'Kids under four, free' it says in *teeny tiny* letters: '(famous people, too!)'. "*See?*" the worker asks.

"I can't believe it!" I say in total disbelief.

"Go have fun at the park!"

"Thanks! I will!" I say as I enter the park. I guess there *are* some perks of being famous!

I realize I don't know where Grace and the girls are, so I pick up my phone and call Grace.

"Hello!" Grace says when she picks up.

"Hi! Where are you?" I ask.

"The girls and I are by the Ferris wheel!"

"Okay! I'm coming!"

"See you in a minute!"

"Bye!" I respond happily as I make my way toward the Ferris wheel.

I look around for Grace and the other girls at the Ferris wheel. I don't see them right away, but I *do* see a small booth surrounded with people! Grace didn't say that they were *at* the Ferris wheel, but she did say that they were *by* the Ferris wheel. So, I decide to go check out the booth.

As I get closer to the booth, I realize that the people surrounding it are: Grace, Christy, Nicolle, and Sabrina! I rush over to them. Before I can say anything, I see Megan sitting in the booth!!! She stands up and gives me an *enormous* hug.

I am too stunned to say anything.

"Victoria!!! I am sooo happy to see you!!!" she blurts as she squeezes me tightly.

"I have been looking *all over* for you!!!" I exclaim. "Did the girls explain our theory on why we think we woke up here, like this?"

"*Yes!!!*" Megan says happily. "How about we compare our day with my notebook?" Megan says as she pulls her notebook out of her duffel bag that's sitting next to her. "Christy, explain to us your morning!"

"I woke up in a house with Dylan Harper, no children, no pets, I'm a fashion designer, and um... oh! I have a Ferrari!" Christy explains.

"What you said is the *exact same* results as in my notebook!" Megan exclaims. "Grace, your turn!"

"I woke up in a house with Flinn Cosman, no pets or kids, and a *red car!* Oh, and I'm a photographer!" Grace says excitedly.

"Nice! I got the same things here! Okay, Nicolle, you go!" Megan continues.

"I woke up with Aaron Ducet in a shack. I'm an actress with one kid, a Jeep, and a turtle." Nicolle tells us.

"Samesies!" Megan sings. "Sabrina! You go!"

"Leo Higgins, house, Honda, pet rabbit!" Sabrina says quickly.

"Kids?" Megan asks.

"Yes! Like three!" Sabrina responds.

Megan nods her head happily. "Victoria, now you!" Megan says.

"I woke up in a mansion with Allister Cookie, a limo, a baby, a cat, and I'm a famous singer!" I exclaim.

"I have the *exact same* results!" Megan says excitedly as she points to her notebook.

Christy looks at Megan. "Tell us about you!" Christy says.

"Okay, so I woke up in a mansion with Kevin Kallard and one child. We have no pets, but we *do* have a nice blue car! I'm also an artist!" Megan explains as she points to the caricatures she had been doing. "I have the same results in my notebook!" Megan laughs just as a really strong gust of wind, blows her notebook out of her hands.

Megan, Christy, Nicolle, Grace, Sabrina, and I all chase after it. After all, Megan's notebook is one of her most prized possessions. Ahead of us I see a person dressed in a cow costume, almost identical to the one I bumped into at Chick-fil-A. Wait no! *Exactly identical!* The cow/person catches

Megan's notebook!

"Oh my goodness! Thank you!" Megan says as she reaches out to get her notebook back. The cow/person stands, frozen in place for a moment, then another insanely strong gust of wind blows the notebook out of the cows hands – *I mean hooves!*

"Like why is it like so windy!?!" Sabrina exclaims.

"Get my notebook!" Megan screams as the cow jets away from us. "I have exactly sixty seven Lizzie McGuire drawings in there!"

The cow just keeps running.

We all run after it.

"Stop!" Nicolle exclaims.

"FOLLOW THAT EVIL COW!!!" Megan screams.

I turn a corner. I don't see any of the girls! I sit down on a bench to catch my breath.

All of a sudden, Grace comes over and sits down next to me, panting.

"Have you seen the others?" she asks in between breaths.

"No, have you?" I ask her.

"No, I haven't!" she says as she takes a big long breath. "I can't run anymore!"

"Neither can I!"

"Where did you look for Megan?"

"First, I went to a place called, 'Do sm'ART'. Then I looked at 'J's ART Palace'. After that, I walked around 'J's P-ART-Y!'. Then I came here to the 'J-musement Park'!"

"Don't you think it's weird that most of the places that you went to have a J in their name?" Grace thinks out loud.

"What do you mean?"

"You know, there's 'J's ART Palace,' and 'J's P-ART-Y!' and 'J-musement Park.' *Oh!* And the 'J. Theatre on 10th Avenue'!"

"But what about the 10?"

"The letter *J* is the *10th* letter in the alphabet!"

"Nice thinking!"

"But what does the J stand for?"

"My limo driver said that his name was J!"

"Then let's go talk to him! He *definitely* knows more about this city than we do!"

"Yes! Let's go!" I say excitedly as we run toward the exit/entrance of the park.

Once Grace and I reach the exit/entrance, we burst through the gates.

I sprint to the limo.

J rolls down his window. "What's up star? You're drenched in sweat!" J says.

I wipe my forehead with my arm. Wow! I am drenched in sweat! Must be all of this running! "My friend Grace and I would like to know the history of this city!" I say.

"What kind of history?" J asks.

"Why does almost *every* street, building, or place have the letter J in its name?" Grace asks politely. "Are they named after *you?*"

"No they aren't named after *me*, they're named after–" he starts as a loud car alarm interrupts him.

"*WHO?*" Grace hollers over the noise.

"They're named after–" he starts again as the car alarm stops and his phone rings. "I've gotta' take this!" he says as he rolls back up his window.

I look at Grace's stumped face.

"I just don't get it!" Grace says.

"Get what?" I ask.

"There has to be a reason for all of these Js. This can't just be a coincidence!"

"That's true!"

"Where would be a good place to look for information?"

"We don't know the city!"

"Wait! Where's your phone?" Grace asks excitedly.

I pull it out.

"Ask Google why there are so many Js!" she says as I look through my apps. I look for the rainbow G icon.

"I don't see Google!" I say in confusion as I hand my phone to Grace.

She swipes through my apps. "All I see is a rainbow J– wait! It's a rainbow J!!!" Grace screams.

I look at the screen of my phone in Grace's hands.

She points at the app with the rainbow J on it.

I tap it. The screen looks just like the Google search screen, except for it reading 'Google' it says 'Joogle'!

Grace starts laughing hysterically. "Joogle!" she says as she keeps laughing.

I start laughing, too. "Okay, let's take a deep breath and stop laughing," I say.

We both take deep breaths, but keep laughing.

After we calm down, Grace looks at me seriously. "How can we look up this town's history, if we don't even know this town's name?" Grace asks with a stumped look on her face.

I think for a minute.

"We don't know this city's name, but the *citizens* do!" I say excitedly. I rush over to a lady waiting in line to buy tickets. "Excuse me!" I say.

"Oh! Hello there!" she responds.

"Will you tell me what the name of this city, um, town is called?"

"I think the name you're looking for is Janessaville!" she responds.

I look at Grace in shock. "Thank you," I say as Grace and I walk away. "How did we not get this before?"

"Um, Victoria," Grace says as a light bulb turns on in her head.

"Yes?" I ask.

"*Janessa was at the sleepover, too!*"

I stop and think for a moment.

"That's true, Janessa *was* at the sleepover," I say.

"Yes..." Grace says as she waits for me to carry on.

"If *she* was the one who made this madness happen, how *did* she do it?" I try to think back at what happened at the sleepover. I remember Grace saying: 'We didn't invite her to the last sleepover, so I thought we should invite her to this one!' Another thing that sticks out to me is that she rolled her eyes at me when she interrupted me in math class. The cow also rolled it's eyes at me when I bumped into it! "Grace!!! Janessa is the evil cow!!!" I exclaim.

Grace looks at me with confusion.

"What do you mean?" she asks.

"In Mr. E's class on Friday he called on me but I zoned out and I couldn't answer. Janessa interrupted and rolled her eyes at me, and the evil cow rolled it's eyes at me too, so Janessa is the evil cow!" I exclaim.

"You don't know if the cow rolled it's eyes at you!" Grace corrects.

"But–" I start as my phone rings. I answer and it's Sabrina!

"Where like are you?" she asks as I pick up.

"I'm outside of the park!" I say.

"Meet like us by the like water rides!"

"Okay, Grace and I are on our way!"

"Coolio! See you like in a minute!"

"Alrighty! Bye!" I say as I hang up.

"Who was *that?*" Grace asks me.

"It was Sabrina! She asked us to meet her by the water rides." I explain.

"Then let's go!" Grace says as we make our way back to the park entrance.

* * * * *

We walk through the turnstile and look around.

I see a little booth with a J-musement Park logo on it. We walk over to it and find maps covering the table. I grab one and open it. Grace and I observe the map. We find a place called 'Water World'.

"We should head to Water World! It's left of the Ferris wheel!" I suggest as we start walking around the park. We find the Ferris wheel, turn left, and see a large banner that reads: 'Water World'.

"Looks like we're in the right place!" Grace says as we survey the area.

There are huge water rides surrounding us with *enormous* splashes. I personally don't *love* water rides with big splashes. At Disneyland I like Pirates of the Caribbean because there is *not* a huge splash. But Splash Mountain on the other hand has a *colossal* splash! I *don't* like that one! The last time I rode Splash Mountain, I sat in the front and got *drenched!*

Grace and I look around and see Nicolle, Christy, Megan, and Sabrina sitting on a bench. We rush over to them.

"Did you get your notebook back?" Grace asks.

"Yes!" Megan says with relief.

"And the best part is that the pages with our M.A.S.H.es on them, are still intact!" Christy exclaims as Megan flips through the pages of her notebook to show us.

"But the thing is, we can't figure out who the evil cow is!" Nicolle says stumped.

"Well, I think I do!" I state.

"Who's the cow?" they ask in unison.

"It's Janessa!" I declare.

"Why do you say *that?*" Nicolle asks.

I explain my hypothesis.

"So what you're like saying is that Janessa is like the cow?" Sabrina asks for clarification.

"Are you sure that the cow you saw at Chick-fil-A is the *same* one that took Megan's notebook?" Christy inquires.

"Where would you find *another* cow?" Grace asks.

"I like don't know!" Sabrina thinks aloud.

"Where did the cow end up?" I ask.

"How did you get the notebook?" Grace asks excitedly.

"We chased the cow, but when we lost it we asked people if they had seen a cow. They pointed us in the right direction. We ended up here! The girls and I cornered the cow. When it tried to get out, we jumped on it and I ripped my notebook out of the cow's hooves!" Megan explains excitedly.

"Nice!" Grace exclaims.

"Where is the cow *now?*" I ask.

The girls look at me in silence.

"Uh, I think I saw it go like that way." Sabrina says as she points toward another part of the park.

"Ugh, how will we be able to find it in this *huge* park?" Megan groans.

"Come on, it won't be *that* hard to find a cow lurking around the park!" Grace reassures us.

* * * * *

I open my map and borrow a magenta pen from Megan. I separate the park into six different sections. We each decide where we will go.

"What do you think? We could each take a portion of the park and if one of us finds the cow, text or call the others and we'll meet at that person's area." I suggest.

All the girls agree to my idea.

"Does everyone have a phone?" Grace asks.

We all nod.

"Great! Let's like go!" Sabrina shouts as we split up.

I walk over to the entrance of my area where there is a large sign hanging up that reads, 'Mythology Land'.

I walk into a small shop called, 'Starfish Stuff'. They sell mermaid scaled backpacks, mermaid shaped puzzle erasers, clothes, toys for pools or bathtubs, beach towels, and swimsuits, *but* no cows.

I walk over to a ride that is a lot like the Dumbo ride at Disneyland, except in place of flying elephants there are pegasi. I look at the people riding it, and the people in line. *No cows.*

I notice a cart that sells unicorn churros. The churros have multicolored sugar. They call them, 'Unicorn Horns'. Apparently the churros are supposed to look like unicorn horns. I can kind of see a resemblance. *Kind of.*

I see a ride called, 'Voyage to Mermaid Cove'. It's a cute little boat ride. I peer at the people in the boats and in the line. *No cows.*

I walk into another store called, 'Unistore'. All they have is unicorn this and unicorn that, so that *definitely* doesn't include cows.

I walk over to a unicorn carousel, an outdoor fairy themed kiddie roller coaster, a fairy themed store, a dragon dark ride, and a dragon themed store. *No cows!*

All this looking is making me thirsty, so I walk over to a 'Fairy Juice Stand'. Maybe if I can get into the park for free, they will give me free juice! And while I'm at it, maybe I can ask if the worker has seen any cows!

"Have you seen a –" I start as I notice that her name tag says 'Janessa'!

"Have I seen a what?" she asks as I pull out my phone and text all the girls to let them know I might have found Janessa! I tell them to come to 'Mythological Land'. In less than ten minutes, all of the girls are at the 'Fairy Juice Stand'.

"Where's the cow!" Megan shouts eagerly.

"*What cow?* I haven't seen one all day." Janessa says sarcastically .

"Oh! *I* know why you haven't seen one!" Megan says slyly.

"Why?" Janessa laughs.

"Because *you* were the one in the cow costume!" Megan declares as she opens up her notebook to the page with Janessa's M.A.S.H. on it. "Here it states that Janessa would marry Deric Jacobs, would live in an apartment with their two children and dog. They would have a Mercedes Benz, and she would work at *Chick-fil-A!*"

"Then why is she working *here?*" Christy inquires.

"And why did she run away from us?" Nicolle asks.

"My thought is that she is an evil cow alien from the planet Mars!" Megan declares.

"*Hey!*" Janessa defends.

"See! She *is!*" Megan screams.

"I'll be right back!" Janessa says as she starts walking away from us.

"Where are *you* going sister?" Megan interrogates as she

stops Janessa.

"I need to go get something!" Janessa says as she dodges Megan, and runs toward the 'Starfish Stuff' shop.

"We like were like so close!" Sabrina grunts.

Megan pulls an eraser out of her pocket and starts erasing Janessa's M.A.S.H.! Once Megan finishes erasing the M.A.S.H., Janessa disappears into thin air!

"Where did she go?" Christy, Grace, Nicolle, Sabrina, and I exclaim, frightened in unison.

"I just erased her M.A.S.H. and she uh... disappeared!?!" Megan stutters.

We all look at her in total confusion.

"*Huh?*" Sabrina asks.

"Do you want me to erase *your* M.A.S.H. to see where she went?" Megan says enthusiastically as she waves her eraser in the air.

"Erase like all our M.A.S.H.es!" Sabrina says courageously, without missing a beat. She stands tall with her shoulders back and puts her arms in the air triumphantly, like she just won a soccer match for the fifth time in a row.

"Okay!" Megan says excitedly as she vigorously erases Sabrina's M.A.S.H. In the blink of an eye Sabrina disappears. I'm blown away, but terrified at the same time. "*Who's next?*" Megan asks as she smiles maniacally.

"Um... I guess I will?" Nicolle says nervously.

Megan erases hers frantically, and Nicolle disappears.

Do I want to stay here, or go into the unknown?

"I kind of like it here." Grace says.

"Me, too!" Christy tells me.

"I kind of like being a famous singer!" I admit.

"Do you want to stay here?" Megan asks. "Or do you want to be erased?"

"I like it here, but I'm nervous to be erased," I say.

"I'm afraid of the unknown, too," Grace admits. "If I get erased, will you do it with me?" she asks.

"Grace, I can just hear your brother saying, 'To be erased or not to be erased, that is the question,'" Christy says. That really *is* the question. "*Wait!* What if Megan erases one of us and then we text each other to let them know we're okay!"

"Okay!" Grace and I say timidly.

"Erase me!" Christy says nervously.

Megan erases, and Christy is gone.

I grab my phone, with my hands shaking. I text:

R U OK?

A few seconds later I get a thumbs up emoji, along with a long message saying that Sabrina, Nicolle, Janessa, and herself are okay.

"Grace," I say as I gather my courage, "Do you want to get erased?"

"I'm not sure!" Grace says nervously.

"I'll do it with you!" I say courageously.

"Megan! Erase us!" Grace says confidently.

One second I'm standing with Grace in an amusement park, and the next I'm in her basement! Suddenly, Megan appears. We're all in our pj's. I look at my hands, they aren't huge. I look down, *they're* gone! Phew!

Tanner comes down the stairs, as the girls and I stand mesmerized at the fact that we're here!

"Tanner, what day is it today?" Grace asks.

"It's Friday," he says casually. "Are you finished with your pizza?"

"Whoa! It's like no time has passed here!" Grace exclaims.

"What do you mean? You *just* finished dinner!" Tanner corrects.

"Cool!" Grace says in awe.

Tanner takes the paper plates, cups, and empty pizza boxes upstairs.

"How did no time pass?" I ask, astonished.

"I should explain myself," Janessa sighs. "When you suggested playing M.A.S.H. I was all in. I love to play pranks and so I thought it would be fun to make you wake up with your M.A.S.H.es! You were all inside the *crazy* place in my mind that I call 'Janessaville'. I was able to transport you all there and have you wake up in your M.A.S.H.es, because I come from a family of witches. We don't especially like the term *witches*, we like *pranksters* better. *I* do at least. *Because* we are witches, we have magic. That's how I was able to transport you to 'Janessaville'.

"My mom can get cranky, and offended easily, for example, if you don't invite me to a sleepover, that's when she goes *all out*!

"Megan, I ran off with your notebook, because I was trying to find an eraser! I wanted to show you that there was a way out of Janessaville! I am *soooooooooooooo* sorry for ruining your sleepover!" Janessa explains.

I run over and give her a hug.

"You didn't ruin the sleepover, you made it even *better!* I *loved* being a singing star! Singing on the stage at the J. Theatre was absolutely *incredible!*" I exclaim.

"It was astonishing to be an actress on a stage in a show!" Nicolle says.

"I used the coolest camera *ever* as a photographer!" Grace declares.

"I didn't really design outfits, but today was absolutely *mind-blowing!*" Christy says very excitedly.

"Babysitting Victoria's baby like was a lot of fun!" Sabrina yelps.

"*Really?*" Janessa asks dumbfounded.

"*Yes!* This sleepover was totes 'mazing!" I tell her.

BOOK THREE IN THE
Sundance Springs Series

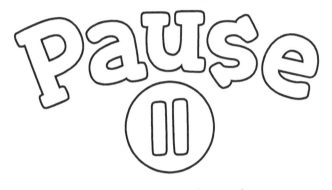

Now Available

· ✦ ✦ · Acknowledgments · ✦ ✦ ·

Special thanks to:

Mom: Thank you for working your magic with my book. You are great at enhancing my ideas by constantly teaching me and encouraging me to stretch my abilities. I am so grateful.

Dad: I treasure all the laughs we've had with my edits. Our mini art lessons have helped me cultivate and improve my art style. When I show you an illustration, you always know just what to say to make sure it's my best.

Caroline: Dude, you make me laugh! And, you help my characters come to life. Things you say, and things we play, movies we watch, things we quote, and all the time we spend together reading has really guided me as a writer and illustrator. I hope you catch the mini Easter Eggs hidden throughout this book for you! You are the most totes 'mazing sister in the WHOLE world!

My Grandparents: Thank you for supporting me, my books, and my imagination. I love that I am able to share my stories with you. GM: I look forward to Chick-fil-a Tuesdays for "no pickles" and keeping a lookout for our favorite cow! PC: It always makes me smile to see my books on your couch. GG: Thanks for sharing my books with everyone on your phone tree. PW: I love that you are always eager to read my books and quiz me about them.

Butler Middle School Staff: Ladena Saxey, Vicki Wilkins, Melissa Christensen, Shandie Holman, Stephanie McDonald, Sara Allen, and Paula Logan. Your positivity keeps me writing. I'm lucky to be a part of the Butler Middle School community. I love being a Bruin.

Readers: Writing for happy, kind, caring, and loving people is what inspires me. Thank you being one of my readers.

J-Musement Park

Victoria is stuck inside the
J-Musement Park. Help her find her way out!

⬇ EXIT ⬇

Word Search

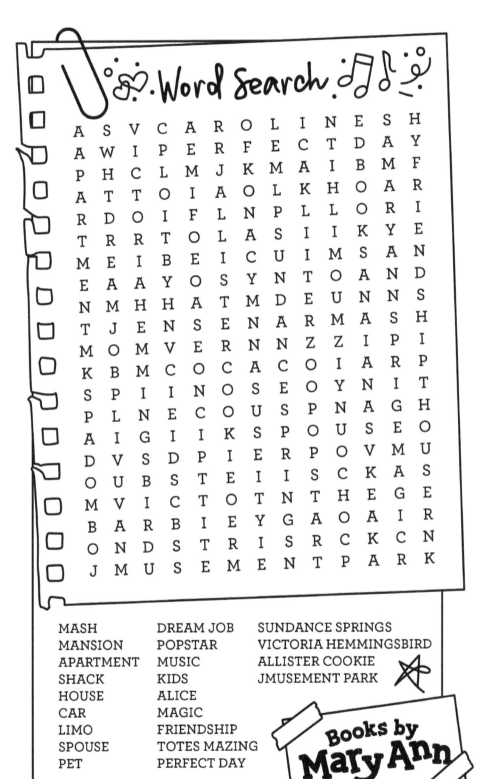

```
A S V C A R O L I N E S H
A W I P E R F E C T D A Y
P H C L M J K M A I B M F
A T T O I A O L K H O A R
R D O I F L N P L L O R I
T R R T O L A S I I K Y E
M E I B E I C U I M S A N
E A A Y O S Y N T O A N D
N M H H A T M D E U N S S
T J E N S E N A R M A S H
M O M V E R N N Z Z I P I
K B M C O C A C O I A R P
S P I I N O S E O Y N I T
P L N E C O U S P N A G H
A I G I I K S P O U S E O
D V S D P I E R P O V M U
O U B S T E I I S C K A S
M V I C T O T N T H E G E
B A R B I E Y G A O A I R
O N D S T R I S R C K C N
J M U S E M E N T P A R K
```

MASH   DREAM JOB   SUNDANCE SPRINGS
MANSION   POPSTAR   VICTORIA HEMMINGSBIRD
APARTMENT   MUSIC   ALLISTER COOKIE
SHACK   KIDS   JMUSEMENT PARK
HOUSE   ALICE
CAR   MAGIC
LIMO   FRIENDSHIP
SPOUSE   TOTES MAZING
PET   PERFECT DAY

Books by Mary Ann

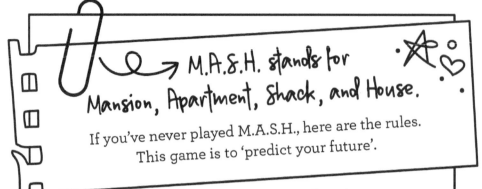

M.A.S.H. stands for Mansion, Apartment, Shack, and House.

If you've never played M.A.S.H., here are the rules. This game is to 'predict your future'.

Fill in Blanks

On the lines, write down three crushes, three cars you want (or colors of cars that you think are cool), numbers of how many kids you want, your favorite animals, and your dream jobs.

Pick a Number

Pick a number between one and ten, and write it in the center circle. This is your lucky number because it will predict your future!

Let's say you picked the number five. You would start at the 'M' in M.A.S.H., counting 'M' as one, 'A' as two, 'S' as three, and 'H' as four, and would then cross out your first crush (since they are number five). You would then start counting again, with your second crush being one, and would continue on and on, going through your cars, kids, pets, jobs, and then back to the top again. Continue doing this until there is only one thing uncrossed item in each category.

Read your Future

The last thing left in each category is what you will read as your 'future.' The crush left will be your spouse, the car left will be your future ride, the number left will be how many kids you'll have, the animal left will be your pet, and the job left will be your future occupation!

Books by Mary Ann

NAME: _____

(MANSION)   (APARTMENT)   (SHACK)   (HOUSE)

SPOUSE
(LIST 3 OF YOUR CRUSHES)

_____

_____

_____

PICK A
NUMBER BETWEEN
1 AND 10

CAR
(LIST 3 CARS YOU WANT)

_____

_____

_____

NUMBER OF KIDS
(HOW MANY KIDS DO YOU WANT? PICK 4 NUMBERS.)

_____   _____   _____   _____

PET
(LIST 3 OF YOUR FAVORITE ANIMALS)

_____

_____

_____

JOB
(LIST 3 OF YOUR DREAM JOBS)

_____

_____

_____

NAME: _____

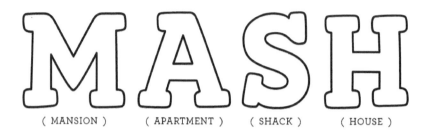

(MANSION)   (APARTMENT)   (SHACK)   (HOUSE)

SPOUSE
(LIST 3 OF YOUR CRUSHES)

_____

_____

_____

PICK A NUMBER BETWEEN 1 AND 10

CAR
(LIST 3 CARS YOU WANT)

_____

_____

_____

NUMBER OF KIDS
(HOW MANY KIDS DO YOU WANT? PICK 4 NUMBERS.)

_____   _____   _____   _____

PET
(LIST 3 OF YOUR FAVORITE ANIMALS)

_____

_____

_____

JOB
(LIST 3 OF YOUR DREAM JOBS)

_____

_____

_____

NAME: _____

(MANSION)   (APARTMENT)   (SHACK)   (HOUSE)

SPOUSE
(LIST 3 OF YOUR CRUSHES)

_____

_____

_____

PICK A
NUMBER BETWEEN
1 AND 10

CAR
(LIST 3 CARS YOU WANT)

_____

_____

_____

NUMBER OF KIDS
(HOW MANY KIDS DO YOU WANT? PICK 4 NUMBERS.)

____   ____   ____   ____

PET
(LIST 3 OF YOUR FAVORITE ANIMALS)

_____

_____

_____

JOB
(LIST 3 OF YOUR DREAM JOBS)

_____

_____

_____

NAME: _____

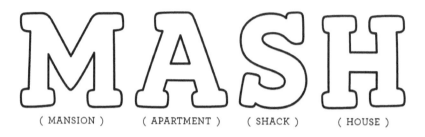

(MANSION)   (APARTMENT)   (SHACK)   (HOUSE)

SPOUSE
(LIST 3 OF YOUR CRUSHES)

_____

_____

_____

PICK A NUMBER BETWEEN 1 AND 10

CAR
(LIST 3 CARS YOU WANT)

_____

_____

_____

NUMBER OF KIDS
(HOW MANY KIDS DO YOU WANT? PICK 4 NUMBERS.)

_____   _____   _____   _____

PET
(LIST 3 OF YOUR FAVORITE ANIMALS)

_____

_____

_____

JOB
(LIST 3 OF YOUR DREAM JOBS)

_____

_____

_____

NAME: _____

(MANSION) (APARTMENT) (SHACK) (HOUSE)

SPOUSE
(LIST 3 OF YOUR CRUSHES)

_____

_____

_____

PICK A
NUMBER BETWEEN
1 AND 10

CAR
(LIST 3 CARS YOU WANT)

_____

_____

_____

NUMBER OF KIDS
(HOW MANY KIDS DO YOU WANT? PICK 4 NUMBERS.)

_____ _____ _____ _____

PET
(LIST 3 OF YOUR FAVORITE ANIMALS)

_____

_____

_____

JOB
(LIST 3 OF YOUR DREAM JOBS)

_____

_____

_____

NAME: _____

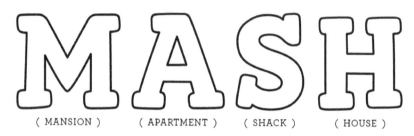

(MANSION) (APARTMENT) (SHACK) (HOUSE)

SPOUSE
(LIST 3 OF YOUR CRUSHES)

_____

_____

_____

PICK A NUMBER BETWEEN 1 AND 10

CAR
(LIST 3 CARS YOU WANT)

_____

_____

_____

NUMBER OF KIDS
(HOW MANY KIDS DO YOU WANT? PICK 4 NUMBERS.)

____ ____ ____ ____

PET
(LIST 3 OF YOUR FAVORITE ANIMALS)

_____

_____

_____

JOB
(LIST 3 OF YOUR DREAM JOBS)

_____

_____

_____